William H. Brown

**The Babylonian Captivity**

William H. Brown

**The Babylonian Captivity**

ISBN/EAN: 9783337235635

Printed in Europe, USA, Canada, Australia, Japan

Cover: Foto ©Andreas Hilbeck / pixelio.de

More available books at **www.hansebooks.com**

THE

# BABYLONIAN CAPTIVITY.

BY

WILLIAM HENRY BROWN, B.A.

*(Member of the Society of Biblical Archæology.)*

---

**SECOND EDITION.**

---

LONDON:

HARRISON AND SONS, ST. MARTIN'S LANE,
Printers in Ordinary to Her Majesty.

1874.

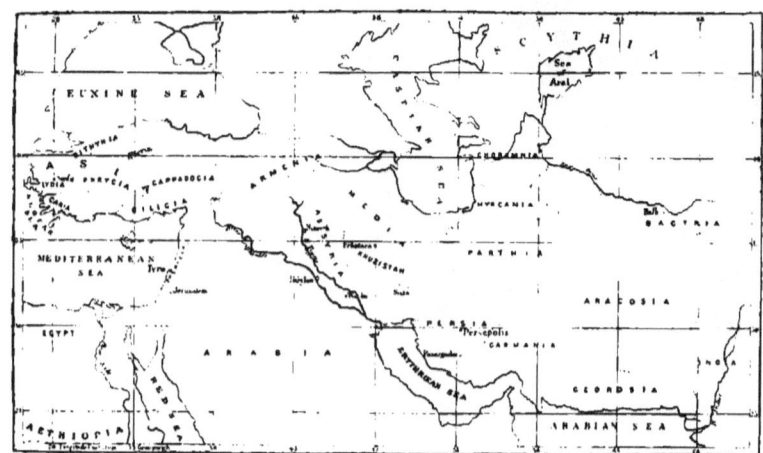

# THE BABYLONIAN CAPTIVITY.

*See the Essay on "Cyrus the Second," in Volume I, Part 2, of the "Transactions of the Society of Biblical Archæology;" by J. W. Bosanquet, F.R.A.S. Also "Messiah the Prince," by the same Author; Longmans and Co.*

BY WILLIAM HENRY BROWN, B.A.

No one who has made the attempt to understand the course of events in the East at the time of the Captivity of the Jews, or to fix the dates of the reigns of Nebuchadnezzar, Belshazzar, and Cyrus the Great, can have failed to be wonderfully perplexed with the difficulty of the subject, and with the number of varying schemes which are met with in different histories and dictionaries. No satisfactory plan has ever yet been hit upon by which to reconcile the conflicting data and names. Nabonidus, king of Babylon, who, according to Berosus, was overthrown by Cyrus, has been supposed to be the same as Belshazzar; whereas recently-discovered inscriptions represent him as his father. Cyrus has always been considered to have been the conqueror of Babylon; and yet we are distinctly told by Daniel that, on the overthrow of her last king, Belshazzar, "Darius the Median took the kingdom."

The Life of Cyrus—commonly called Cyrus the Great—has come down to us written by Herodotus, "the father of history," and by Xenophon in his Cyropædeia. The former represents Cyrus as meeting with his death when invading the territories of the Massagetæ in Scythia; whereas the latter describes him as dying happily amidst his sorrowing children and friends.

It has been a favourite plan with a long series of modern writers to look upon the stories of antiquity as a "tissue of fables," and to reject a great part of the writings of Daniel, Livy, and others, as being unable to bear the test of a subjection to our present "superior enlightenment." Thus the stories of Herodotus have been spoken of as "choice readings," while the Cyropædeia of Xenophon has been thrown aside as a "historical romance" quite unreliable. Recent investigations, however, have done much to give credence to many of the semi-traditional stories of the ancients. In respect to the truthfulness of these writers, the learned author of the article on "Cyrus the Second" justly observes :—

"No such historians ever sat down seriously to record as fact what they knew to be untrue. However much they may have been deceived, they have endeavoured to relate events as they believed them to have occurred, and they are entitled to be heard. It is most unreasonable, when pointed out that Ctesias contradicts Herodotus on several important points of Persian history, complacently to set aside his testimony with the remark, that the authority of Ctesias carries little weight as compared with that of Herodotus: when Xenophon, after careful inquiry, relates in a consistent manner a perfectly different story from that of Herodotus concerning Cyrus, to say with Cicero, or Niebuhr, or with Grote, that Xenophon is evidently writing only political romance: that the testimony of Cleitarchus, Onesicritus, and Megasthenes is spurious and untrustworthy: and as regards the invaluable testimony of Daniel and Ezra, that the evidence of the one is either forgery, or history irreconcilable with secular records, and that of the other has been incorrectly copied."

The story of the Fall of Nineveh, of the supremacy of Babylon under Nebuchadnezzar, of the conquest of Babylon by the Medes and Persians, and finally of the establishment of the Persian Empire under the "Great Kings,"—is derived from many sources. Herodotus, Xenophon, and Ctesias, amongst the ancient Greeks, lived at times not very remote from those days; and many subsequent historians, both before and after the Christian era, have attempted to chronicle those histories. Eastern writings and tradition tell us something, also; and, quite recently, the deciphering of the monuments of Egypt, Nineveh, and Babylon, has given us some precise and reliable authority. But, in addition to these, and as interesting as the accurate information of the cuneiform tablets and cylinders, is the testimony of Daniel the Jew, who lived during the greater part of a long life in or near the city of Babylon, amidst the very scenes as they were transpiring, and was witness of the long struggle of Babylon against the rising power of the Medes and Persians.

To reconcile the apparently varying statements of these authorities, and to adapt them to a chronology which will most nearly agree with the knowledge that we possess, is the province of the archæologist.

The present essay is written, not with the intention of examining or criticising the conclusions of the learned Treasurer of the Society of Biblical Archæology—such a course can only be attempted by a profound student in Asiatic historical research—but to attempt to exhibit his historical theory and his conclusions in a form somewhat more adapted to the general reader, with some additional authorities from ancient sources in support of the general argument. The subject, moreover, is one of equal interest to the student of ancient history and to the reader of the Sacred Books.

The period comprised is that which divides the History of the World before the Christian era into its two natural parts—separating the history of the

ancient monarchies of the East from that of the influence and conquests of Greece and Rome. For it
commences with the Fall of Nineveh in the year 583,
B.C. (according to the new reckoning), and closes with
the final overthrow of the independence of Babylon
by the kings of the Persian Empire, who came in
contact on the shores of the Ægean Sea with the
descendants of the conquerors of Troy, and afterwards
led their innumerable hosts across the Hellespont to
be overthrown at Marathon and Salamis.

———

To make the subject more clear, it will be well to
give the outlines of the *commonly-accepted* history of
*Cyrus the Great*.

The province of Persia, although possessing a native
dynasty of kings, had for a long time been subject to
Media. In B.C. 558, Cyrus the Great, king of Persia,
son of a previous king Cambyses, rebelled against his
suzerain Astyages, king of Media, dethroned him, and
thus founded the great empire of Persia. In 546, he
defeated Crœsus, king of Lydia, took the city of
Sardis, and conquered the whole of Asia Minor. In
538, he took Babylon, overthrowing her last king,
Belshazzar, and placing "Darius the Median" (Daniel
v. 31) as regent over the conquered kingdom ; and,
shortly afterwards, in 536, he issued his famous decree
allowing the Jews to return to their own country. In
529 he died, leaving his great empire to his son
Cambyses.

Thus there are five important events connected
with this king, as represented to us :—

1, the conquest of Media ;
2, the conquest of Lydia ;
3, the conquest of Babylon ;
4, the return of the Jews from captivity ;
5, the death of Cyrus,

(1). The rebellion of Cyrus against Astyages, king of Media, and the transference of supremacy from the Medes to the Persians, is mentioned by Herodotus ; but Xenophon, in his Cyropædeia, is silent about it. On the contrary, Xenophon represents Cyrus as achieving his great victories over Lydia and Babylon, whilst his father Cambyses was king of Persia, and Cyaxares was king of Media ; as marrying the daughter of Cyaxares, receiving all Media as her dowry, and succeeding Cyaxares on the throne of Media.

(2). The conquest of Crœsus, king of Lydia, and capture of Sardis, is mentioned by both Herodotus and Xenophon.

(3). The conquest of Babylon is mentioned by Herodotus and Xenophon, and is incidentally referred to by Daniel (vi. 28) and Ezra (v. 13).

(4). Respecting the return of the Jews from Babylon, Cyrus is named by Isaiah (xliv. 28) and is distinctly mentioned by Ezra, as issuing the Decree permitting the Jews to return to the land of their fathers, and to rebuild the Temple of their God.

(5). Lastly, Herodotus tells us that Cyrus was killed in battle, while Xenophon represents him as dying peacefully, and giving his last injunctions to his children. The Mohammedan writer, Tabari, agrees with Herodotus ; for he speaks of " Kai-Khosru (Cyrus), who, having appointed Lohrasp (Cambyses) his successor, suddenly disappeared, so that no trace of him could ever be discovered."

From these important differences, combined with other evidence, it appears probable that Herodotus and Xenophon have mixed up two separate kings. The general portrait of Cyrus, as represented by these two historians, bears hardly any agreement ; and Herodotus seems, in most respects, to have written about one king Cyrus, while Xenophon wrote about another Cyrus, his grandson. They will now be respectively called

*Cyrus the First* and
*Cyrus the Second.*[*]

The altered chronology has been based upon a careful comparison of all the sources from which we derive the history of these times, as well as upon the calculations of the eclipses which are recorded as having been observed at Babylon and other places. The Eclipse of Thales (Herodotus i. 74), which forms the key to a large portion of the chronology, is now decided, upon the authority of the Astronomer Royal, to have occurred in the year 585, and not in the year 610; and thus many of the dates within a certain period have been brought about twenty-five years nearer to the Christian era. A number of tribute-tablets in the cuneiform character, found at Babylon and Warka, giving with great precision the regnal date of each tribute and the name of the king, have lent much aid in unravelling the discrepancies of historians. The original arrangement of these tablets, however, was lost, when they were dug up and sent to this country ; so that they do not inform us positively as to the order of succession of the kings, although they tell us the number of years of each reign. By an arrangement of these tablets according to the chronology of the Jewish historian Demetrius, instead of according to that of the Alexandrian astronomer Ptolemy, much light seems thrown upon the history of these times. It is hardly to be supposed that every difficulty can be disposed of and dispersed by this altered reckoning; but, as will be seen, it clears away

---

[*] As Cyrus the Second was not one of the successors of Cyrus the First, these two kings are written Cyrus *the First* and Cyrus *the Second.* On the other hand, Cyaxares II. was one of the successors of Cyaxares I., and they are written (with the Roman numerals) Cyaxares I. and Cyaxares II.

very much that was previously quite irreconcilable, and we may reasonably expect that the future deciphering of the cuneiform inscriptions from Babylon and its neighbourhood will still further corroborate the main features of the new arrangement.

The destruction of Nineveh is thought to have taken place in the year 583. For, although the Assyrian empire came to an end in the year 610, yet that was the year in which Sardanapalus, king of Nineveh and Babylon, became subject to the Scythians, who from that time held the sway over Assyria for 28 years (Herodotus i. 103—106, and iv. 1). Sardanapalus is the king who is also called Nabuchodonosor (Book of Judith), Labynetus I. (Herodotus i. 74), and Nabopalassar. After a time he transferred his residence to Babylon, when the Scythians probably placed Saracus as their vassal on the throne of Nineveh. In the year 583, Nabopalassar formed an alliance with Cyaxares I., king of Media, and the joint armies of the Babylonians and Medes drove the Scythians from Asia and destroyed the city of Nineveh.

It will be seen that Cambyses, the father of Cyrus, and Cambyses, the successor of Cyrus and conqueror of Egypt, are now supposed to be one and the same king; that two new kings, Cyaxares II. and Cyrus the Second, take their places in history; and that "Darius the Median" (Daniel v. 31)—whom modern historians have been obliged to consider as some unknown prince appointed by Cyrus as his Viceroy on the throne of Babylon for about two years—is no other than Darius, son of Hystaspes, who finally united and consolidated the Medo-Persian empire.

Let us now divide the *newly-arranged* history into two parts,

I. MEDIA AND PERSIA,
II. BABYLON AND THE JEWS,

with tables at the beginning of each part, exhibiting *the old and new systems of history and chronology.*

## I. Media and Persia.

| OLD DATE. | | EVENTS, AS COMMONLY ARRANGED. |
|---|---|---|
| 610 | .. | Eclipse of Thales. |
| 606 | .. | Nineveh destroyed by the Babylonians and Medes. |
| 604 | .. | Nebuchadnezzar, King of Babylon. |
| 594 | .. | Astyages, King of Media. |
| 560 | .. | Crœsus, King of Lydia. |
| 558 | .. | Cyrus, King of Persia. |
| 558 | .. | Cyrus conquered Media. |
| 546 | .. | Cyrus conquered Lydia. |
| 538 | .. | Cyrus conquered Babylon. |
| 536 | .. | Cyrus issued the Decree. |
| 529 | .. | Cambyses, King of Persia. |
| 525 | .. | Cambyses conquered Egypt. |
| 522 | .. | Gomates (Pseudo-Smerdis), King of Persia. |
| 521 | .. | Darius I., King of Persia. |
| | | Suppression of rebellions in Babylon. |
| 490 | | Battle of Marathon. |

---

| NEW DATE. | | EVENTS, ACCORDING TO THE NEW ARRANGEMENT. |
|---|---|---|
| 585 | .. | Eclipse of Thales. |
| 583 | .. | Nineveh destroyed by the Babylonians and Medes. |
| 581 | .. | Nebuchadnezzar, King of Babylon. |
| 574 | .. | Astyages, King of Media. |
| 566 | .. | Cyrus the First, King of Persia. |
| 559 | .. | Cyrus the First acquired the supremacy over Media. |
| 549 | .. | Crœsus, King of Lydia. |
| 539 | .. | Cyaxares II., vassal-King of Media. |
| 536 | .. | Death of Cyrus the First when Darius was scarce 20 years old.* |
| 536 | .. | Cambyses succeeded Cyrus the First. |
| 535 | .. | Conquest of Asia-Minor (Lydia) by Cyrus the Second. |
| 530 | .. | First conquest of Babylon by Cyrus the Second. |

---

* Herod i. 209.

| NEW DATE. | EVENTS, ACCORDING TO THE NEW ARRANGEMENT. |
|---|---|
| 525 .. | Cambyses conquered Egypt. |
| 525 .. | Cyrus the Second succeeded Cyaxares II. |
| 522 .. | Revolt of Darius in Persia. |
| 518 .. | Gomates (Pseudo-Smerdis), King of Persia. |
| 517 .. | Darius, King of Persia. |
| 513 . | Cyrus the Second " King of Babylon." |
| 513 | Decree of Cyrus. |
| 506 .. | Darius succeeded Cyrus the Second at Babylon. |
| 498 .. | Association of Xerxes, called Ahasuerus,* in the government of the empire. |
| 493 .. | Final conquest of Babylon by Darius when about 62 years old.† |
| 490 .. | Battle of Marathon. |
| 486 .. | Xerxes, King of Persia. |
| 484 .. | Death of Darius, at the age of 72.‡ |

## THE HISTORY OF MEDIA AND PERSIA.

### (ACCORDING TO THE NEW ARRANGEMENT.)

In the year 583, when *Nabopalassar* was king of Babylon and *Cyaxares 1.* was king of Media, the Babylonians and Medes destroyed the city of Nineveh; and Saracus, who had been placed on the throne as the vassal of the Scythians, destroyed himself amidst the flames of his palace. The mighty Assyrian Empire came to an end, after having held the supremacy in the East for many centuries. The province of Assyria was added to the vast dominions of the king of Media, and became his westernmost territory. The western portion of the Assyrian Empire, including the subjugated districts around Palestine, fell to the lot of the king of Babylon.

In 581, *Nebuchadnezzar* succeeded his father Nabopalassar. The city of Babylon is believed to have been older than the city of Nineveh; but for a long

---

* Ezra iv. 6.        † Dan. v. 31.        ‡ Ctesias.

time the kings of Babylon had been subject to the
kings of Assyria, with intervals during which they
enjoyed their independence. Thus, during many centuries, with but little interruption, Assyria held the
supremacy (or hegemony) in the East. After the
destruction of Nineveh, however, Babylon again became independent, and the *Babylonian or Chaldæan
Empire* began its short though brilliant career. There
were now four great monarchies :—Egypt, Babylon,
Media, and Lydia. Nebuchadnezzar reigned forty-
three years until 538, and was succeeded by his son
Evil-merodach.

In the meantime, during the long reign of Nebuchadnezzar at Babylon, great changes occurred in the
countries east of the valley of the Tigris and Euphrates.
Hitherto the sons of Shem and of Ham had held the
glory of imperial power. The decendants of Ham
had filled the narrow valley of the Nile with a mighty
nation ; those of Shem had set up their empire in the
valley of the Tigris and Euphrates. Now, for the first
time in the history of mankind, the sons of Japhet
were to come forth to conquer, and to add the valleys
of the Euphrates and the Nile to their dominions.
The Tigris-Euphrates valley is bordered on the east
by a long range of mountains, which form the western
edge of the great table-land of *Iran* (embracing the
modern Persia, Affghanistan, and Beloochistan),
stretching across from the valley of the Tigris on
the one side to that of the Indus on the other.

Here was the original home of the great Indo-
European race ; and the *Medes and Persians*, who
inhabited the most westerly portions of this table-
land and bordered on the dominions of Nineveh and
Babylon, were sprung from the *Aryan* branch of this
family. The religion of the Aryan race was monotheistical, somewhat resembling that of the Jews, and
purer than the polytheism of the Semitic nations.

This religion was afterwards reformed by Zoroaster. The Medes and the Persians had many institutions in common. The Medes had shaken off the yoke of the kings of Assyria, and had long been an independent kingdom. The Persians had kings of their own, but they were tributary to the kings of Media.

In 566, *Cyrus the First*, of the royal family of Achæmenes, succeeded to the throne of Persia. In 559, he overthrew *Astyages*, king of Media, and, transferring the supremacy of the two nations from Media to Persia, he has been commonly considered as the founder of the Persian or Medo-Persian Empire.

The dominions of Media extended over a vast country, as far as the river Oxus in the north, and to the borders of India in the east. Thus Cyrus was supreme ruler over the whole country from the Tigris-Euphrates valley to the borders of India. He perished, as Herodotus tells us, whilst fighting against the Massagetæ, a tribe of people who inhabited the district around the sea of Aral.

During the reign of Cyrus, in 561, and before his conquest of Media, his son *Cambyses* had married *Mandane*, daughter of Astyages; and in 559, after the overthrow of Astyages, Cyrus himself (according to the authority of Ctesias) married *Amytis*, another and a younger daughter of the same king.

Now *Cyrus the Second* was the son of Cambyses and Mandane, and the grandson of Cyrus the First; and he is really the king who, being of both Persian and Median birth, is said by Megasthenes and Herodotus (i. 55 and 91) to have been foretold to both Nebuchadnezzar and Crœsus as Cyrus "the Mule," who would come to overthrow the kingdoms of Babylon and Lydia. This confounding of the grandfather with the grandson has produced all the discrepancies in the story of the birth of Cyrus. For

Herodotus tells us that Cyrus was the grandson of Astyages (i. 75), which is true of Cyrus the Second ; he tells us also that Cyrus was the son of Cambyses and Mandane (i. 111), which is also true of Cyrus the Second ; and that Cambyses, king of Persia, who conquered Egypt, was the son of Cyrus, which is true of Cyrus the First : and so, historians have hitherto been obliged to suppose that two kings, Cyrus and Cambyses, preceded Cyrus the Great on the vassal-throne of Persia. Ctesias informs us that Cyrus was not related to Astyages until he married his daughter Amytis, which is true of Cyrus the First ; while Xenophon calls Cyrus the grandson of Astyages, which is true of Cyrus the Second (Cyrop. i. 2, 1).

On the death of Cyrus (the First) in 536 (old date 529), his dominions were divided between his two sons *Cambyses* and *Cyaxares II.* Cambyses, the elder, was the son of Cyrus and Cassandane, and was descended, as Herodotus tells us, both through his father and his mother, from the Persian royal family of Achæmenes (Herod. ii. 1, and iii. 2). He therefore received the hereditary kingdom of Persia with the western or Syrian dominions, and is rightly reckoned as the second king of the Persian empire. In addition to this, he inherited the supremacy over Media which his father had acquired. Cyaxares II. (or Tany-axares, or Tany-oxarces), the younger son, is said by Ctesias to have been the son of Cyrus and Amytis, and was therefore the half-brother of Cambyses. As Cyrus did not marry Amytis until after the marriage of his elder son Cambyses with her sister Mandane, Cyaxares was much younger than his brother, and could not have been more than twenty-two years old on the death of Cyrus. Thus, being through his mother the grandson of Astyages, he was of Median birth, and to him, therefore, Cyrus gave the kingdom of Media with the eastern provinces, thus allowing him to sit upon the throne of his grandfather Astyages.

Herodotus says that on the death of Cyrus, Cambyses succeeded to the kingdom (Herod. ii. 1). Ctesias relates that Cyrus left the kingdom to his elder son Cambyses, and appointed his younger son, Tany-oxarces (Cyaxares II.), ruler over the eastern provinces of the empire. Xenophon tells us that Cyrus divided his dominions between his two sons, Cambyses and Tany-axares (Cyaxares II.), giving the "*kingdom*" (*i.e.* Persia, which had acquired the supremacy) to the elder one, and the "*satrapy* of the Medes, Armenians, and Cadusians" to the younger (Cyrop. viii., 7, 11). Thus in the circumstance of the peaceful and happy death of Cyrus, Xenophon appears to be writing of Cyrus the Second; but in the circumstance of the bequest of his dominions to his two sons, he appears to be writing of Cyrus the father of Cambyses. The conjunction of these two circumstances in the death-bed speech of Cyrus to his children, is to be accounted for by attributing it to the supposition that Xenophon, having heard that Cyrus (the First) divided his dominions between his two sons, and having heard also that Cyrus (the Second), his hero, died a natural death, put into his mouth this parting address, abounding in so many sage maxims.

Thus Media and Persia were separated, after having been, as is commonly supposed, united in 559 by the overthrow of Astyages. But were they yet united under one monarchy? Doubtless there took place— what was so common in the history of these nations— a *transfer of supremacy* from Media to Persia. Media, however, was the most extensive of the two kingdoms, and the most important, and the joint customs of the two nations were commonly known as the "laws of the Medes and Persians." Herodotus says that

"Cyrus kept Astyages with him till he died, without doing him any further injury;" and we may suppose that Astyages remained king of Media after he had been "deposed" from the supremacy, which was transferred to Persia; that he reigned thirty-five years in all until his death, and not thirty-five years before he was conquered; and that he died in 539, and was succeeded by Cyaxares II., his grandson. The fact of Cyrus allowing his younger son to sit upon the throne of Media, as is thus supposed, three years before his own death, does not at all interfere with the account already given of the division of his kingdom.

In the Cyropædeia, Xenophon represents Cyaxares II., king of Media, as being the son of Astyages, and as succeeding his father on the throne (Cyrop. i. 5, 2). So that, by his mistake in supposing that there was only one king Cyrus, he first of all tells us that Cyaxares, king of Media, was the father-in-law of Cyrus—thus writing what was true of Cyrus the Second; and afterwards he describes the younger son of Cyrus, under the name Tany-axares (another form of the word Cyaxares)—thus writing what was probably true of Cyrus the First (Cyrop. viii. 5, 28, and viii. 7, 11). Ctesias also agrees with Xenophon in speaking of the younger son of Cyrus by the slightly altered name of Tany-oxarces.

In the year 539, then, *Cyaxares II.*—whether he was the grandson of Astyages and the younger son of Cyrus, or whether he was the son of Astyages—succeeded to the vassal-throne of Media three years before the death of Cyrus. This king is the king *Ahasuerus*, spoken of in the Book of Esther, who reigned from India to Susiana. Respecting this king we are informed (Esther i. 1) that he was "Ahasuerus, who reigned from India even unto *Cush*"—this Cush being the Asiatic Cush, otherwise called Cossæa, Susiana or Khuzistan; and not the

c

African Cush or Æthiopia, as our translators have rendered it. Three years afterwards, in 536, Cyrus died ; and " in those days when the king Ahasuerus sat on the throne of his kingdom, which was in Shushan (Susa) the palace (*i.e.*, came into full possession of his kingdom), in the third year of his reign (*i.e.*, in the third year after the death of Astyages, whom he succeeded as vassal-king), he made a feast unto all his princes and servants " (Esther i. 2—3).

This king Cyaxares II. is referred to several times in Dr. Smith's Dictionaries, and he is always dismissed as having never really existed—one of the articles in those Dictionaries telling us that " the Cyaxares II. of Xenophon is an invention of that amusing writer." He is now supposed to be spoken of under several different names—*Ahasuerus* in the Bible, *Cyaxares* in one part of Xenophon's work, *Tany-axares* in another part, and *Tany-oxarces* by Ctesias. In addition to these names, he might also be called *Xerxes* ; for the names Ahasuerus, Cyaxares, and Xerxes are acknowledged to be the same name written respectively according to the Hebrew, Median and Greek orthographies ; and thus Cyaxares I., the conqueror of Nineveh, is also spoken of in the Book of Tobit (xiv. 15) under the name of Assuerus.

In the year 536, *Cambyses* became king of Persia, and Suzerain over Media. In the year 529 he became also king of Babylon, when that city had been conquered for him (as will be afterwards told) by his son, Cyrus the Second, acting as his lieutenant. This year, 529, has been the commonly received date of his accession, on the supposition that Cyrus, who took Babylon, was his father. In 525, Cambyses undertook the conquest of Egypt, and from that time commences his reign on the throne of the Pharaohs. He remained the *de jure* king of the Persian monarchy until his death, but after setting out on his expedition to Egypt he never reached home again. During his long absence in that country, an almost universal revolt took place in his dominions ; for Persia and Babylon rebelled against him, while the Medes threw off the supremacy which had been imposed upon them by the Persians.

Thus we can explain the different reckonings of the reign of Cambyses. According to Ctesias he reigned eighteen years, from 536 until his death in 518 ; according to Herodotus (iii. 66) he reigned seven years and five months, from 529, when he became king of Babylon, until 522, when Darius, son of Hystaspes, revolted and seized upon the the province of Persia (as will be afterwards mentioned) ; and, according to the Egyptian historian, Manetho, he conquered Egypt in the fifth year of his reign over the Persians (reckoned from the time when he became king of Babylon), and reigned as king of Egypt for six years, from 525 until his death in 518, when he was succeeded by Darius.

Whilst Cambyses was reigning as king of Persia, and Cyaxares II. was reigning as vassal-king of Media (as we are told by Xenophon throughout the Cyropædeia), *Cyrus the Second* son of Cambyses and Mandane, and grandson of Cyrus the First, appears as a conqueror at the age of about twenty-five. Xenophon tells us that when only twelve years old he went with his mother on a visit to his grandfather Astyages, king of Media, that he remained several years at the court of Astyages, and that after his first victories he never returned to Persia, except on occasional visits. From a comparison of the biography of Xenophon with several other sources, we are led to believe that the following are the chief outlines of the life of

Cyrus the Second.   In 535, *Crœsus*, king of Lydia,
invaded Media.  The young Cyrus, on account of
his military talents, was placed at the head of the
united armies of Media and Persia, and acting as the
lieutenant of his father Cambyses, King of Persia,
and of his uncle Cyaxares II., King of Media, he
met the powerful king of Lydia at the battle of
Pteria, and completely overthrew him, afterwards
capturing the city of ·Sardis, his capital.  Crœsus
seems to have lived with his conqueror, and to have
been treated by him as a friend.*  Cyrus was allowed
to rule as king over the dominions which he had
conquered—comprising Asia Minor, Armenia, and
other countries—and to hold his court at Ecbatana
(or Achmetha, Ezra vi. 2 ; Herodotus i. 153) in
Media ; while Cyaxares lived at Susa (or Shushan,
Esther i. 2), and Cambyses held his court at Pasargadæ in Persia.  This great conquest was amongst
the most important of the achievements of Cyrus
the Second ; for the dominions of the Perso-Median
Empire were thus extended to the borders of the
Ægean Sea, and the territory of the king of Babylon
was confined to Syria and the Euphrates Valley.
Well might the tomb of Cyrus bear upon it the
inscription which was noticed by the historian Arrian:
—" I am Cyrus, the son of Cambyses, who acquired
empire for the Persians, and reigned over Asia" (the
modern Asia-Minor).  A few years after the overthrow of Crœsus, Cyrus the Second, again command-
ing the united armies of the Medes and Persians,
took Babylon in the year 530, and put an end to the

---

* Herodotus appears to have been confused when he describes
Crœsus as accompanying Cyrus (the First) in his fatal expedition
against the Massagetæ, but is probably correct in asserting that
he accompanied Cambyses to Egypt.

   It may be mentioned here that a careful investigation of the
chronology of the Kings of Lydia points to the year 534 as the
date of the capture of Sardis, instead of the year 546.

short reign of the young king, Laborosoarchod. Babylon was henceforth considered as a subject province of the empire of Cambyses, and accordingly the year 529 (the year after its capture) counts as the first year of *Cambyses* as king of Babylon. In accordance with the Persian custom, *Nabonidus*, a native Babylonian prince, was appointed satrap or viceroy of Cambyses at Babylon. Cambyses was thus the first of the Persian, or Achæmenian, kings of Babylon ; and on the Babylonian tribute-tablets he bears the double title of " King of Babylon " and "King of the Two Nations" (*i.e.*, king of the two confederate nations of the Medes and the Persians), while Nabonidus bears the title of " King of Babylon " only. During the absence of Cambyses in Egypt, Nabonidus set himself up as an independent sovereign, but the years of his reign were reckoned from the time of his first appointment as viceroy. Thus after this first conquest of Babylon by Cyrus, he did not himself rule at Babylon. For this great victory Cyrus received many honours. Cyaxares promised him his daughter in marriage, and "with her," said he, " I give all Media as her dowry, for I have no legitimate male issue."[*] Before his marriage, however, Cyrus went to Persia to receive the consent of his father. Cambyses received him in presence of the whole Persian court, to whom he spoke : " You, Persians, in case anyone attempts to put an end to Cyrus's empire, or excite any of his subjects to revolt, shall yield such assistance in defence of yourselves and of Cyrus as he shall order" (Xenophon, Cyr. viii. 5, 25) ; thus showing that Cyrus already held a kingdom of his own, which embraced Asia Minor,

---

[*] It is worth mentioning that Xenophon tells us : " There are some authors who say that he married his mother's sister." Now, Cyrus the First, as has been related, did marry Amytis who was the sister of Mandane.

Armenia, and the surrounding countries. On the
death of Cyaxares, who, according to Ctesias, was
compelled to drink poison by his brother Cambyses,
about the year 525, *Cyrus the Second,* his son-in-law,
succeeded to the greater part of his dominions. He
thus became king over the whole country stretching
across from the Ægean Sea on the west to India on
the east, and from the Oxus on the north to the
borders of Syria, Babylon, and Persia on the south;
while Cambyses was the king of Persia, Babylon,
Syria, and Egypt. From this time the Medes seem
to have thrown off the supremacy of Persia, which
had been imposed upon them by Cyrus the First,
and which Cambyses was unable to maintain during
his absence in Egypt.* This independence of Media
was probably upheld by Cyrus the Second until his
death, although his rule over Susiana and other portions of his dominions adjoining to Persia was inter-
rupted by the usurpation of Pseudo-Smerdis, and
afterwards by the rising power of Darius. In 513,
Cyrus marched against Babylon for the second time,
overthrew king *Nabonidus,* and himself assumed the

---

* With regard to this undoubted rising of the Medes against
the supremacy of the Persians, we are confronted with the difficulty of identifying the prince who is called *Smerdis* by Herodotus
and *Bardiya* (Bardes) in the Behistun incription. The narrative
of Herodotus and the inscription on the rock of Behistun agree
in asserting that Smerdis (or Bardes) was the brother of Cambyses, being born of the same father and mother, and that he
was secretly slain by Cambyses; but Herodotus tells us that the
murder was accomplished by a messenger sent from Egypt for
that purpose, while the Behistun inscription relates that it took
place before the expedition to Egypt. Ctesias tells us that
Tany-oxarces (Cyaxares II.) was also put to death by Cambyses.
We cannot assert that Cyaxares II. and Smerdis were one and
the same prince. Yet the power which Gomates the Magian
(Pseudo-Smerdis) acquired by his pretending to be the lost
prince, leads us to suppose that Smerdis must have been of some
importance.

title of " King of Babylon," at the same time issuing
*the Decree or Proclamation* allowing the Jews to
return to Jerusalem and to rebuild the Temple
(Ezra i. 1 ; v. 13 ; vi. 3). His reign as king of
Babylon counts from the year 513, and he reigned
seven years, until his death in 506. On the Babylonian tribute-tablets he also bears the double title
of " King of Babylon " and " King of the Two
Nations." In the Bible he is once, and once only,
styled " king of Babylon " (Ezra v. 13).

Thus Cyrus the Second was essentially a Median
monarch, and never ruled over the hereditary province of Persia. A confirmation of this is furnished
by the accuracy with which Xenophon tells us (Cyr.
viii. 6, 22) that, after his conquests, the royal residences were Babylon, Susa, and Ecbatana—not one
of these cities being in Persia, whose capital at that
time was Pasargadæ.

To return now to the kingdom of Persia. During
the long absence of Cambyses in Egypt (from which
country he never returned, dying on his way home in
Syria), several provinces of his empire revolted
against the supremacy of the Persians. *Darius, son
of Hystaspes,* of the younger branch of the Persian
royal family of Achæmenes, is said by Herodotus to
have been amongst the princes who accompanied
Cambyses in his expedition. He probably returned
in order to uphold the empire, but the continued
absence of Cambyses induced him to revolt, and he
seized the hereditary throne of Persia in 522. From
this time Cambyses was really king only of Egypt,
where he himself was with his army. Darius, son of
Hystaspes, or *Darius I.,* claimed the throne then by
revolt, until the death of Cambyses in 518. In this
year *Gomates the Magian,* called also *Pseudo-Smerdis,*
appears as a successful usurper on the throne of
Persia for seven months. After the death of Go-

mates in 517, Darius held the throne of Persia, and reigned until the year 486, when he was succeeded by his son Xerxes.

The reign of Darius counts sometimes from 522, the year of his successful revolt, and sometimes from 518, after Pseudo-Smerdis had been put to death. At the time of his revolt he also seized upon the province of Babylon, which formed part of the dominions of Cambyses under the viceroy Nabonidus ; and his reign as king of Babylon dates, on some of the Babylonian tablets, from the same year (522) as his revolt in Persia. In 517, Nabonidus seems to have driven Darius from Babylon, and Cyrus afterwards expelled Nabonidus ; and for twelve years (from 517 to 506) the name of Darius seems to be almost unknown on Babylonian tablets. In the year 506, on the death of Cyrus the Second, king of the Medes, of Asia-Minor, and of Babylon, Darius occupied those countries, and the two kingdoms of Media and Persia became united under one monarchy. In the year 493 he finally conquered Babylon, which had again revolted, and " took the kingdom " of Babylon, " being about threescore and two years old " (Daniel v. 31). From the year 493, his title as King of Babylon was finally established, and he became " king over the realm of the Chaldeans " (Daniel ix. 1).

From this time (493) the great *Persian or Medo-Persian Empire* was finally established, and reached the furthest extent of its limits, from the Grecian waters of the Ægean Sea to the borders of India, and from the river Oxus to the south of Egypt and the deserts of Arabia. The dominions of the great monarchies of Assyria, Babylon, Media, Lydia, and Egypt were now united under the Persian Empire by the "Great King;" and, with the exception of Egypt, the empire remained nearly of the same extent until its overthrow by Alexander the Great.

## II. Babylon and the Jews.

| OLD DATE. | EVENTS, AS COMMONLY ARRANGED. |
|---|---|
| 606 | Nineveh destroyed by the Babylonians and and Medes. |
| 608 | Jehoiakim, King of Judah. |
| 605 | Nebuchadnezzar takes Jerusalem the first time—Daniel led captive. |
| 605 | Commencement of the Seventy Years. |
| 604 | Nebuchadnezzar, King of Babylon. |
| 597 | Nebuchadnezzar takes Jerusalem the second time—Jehoiachin (or Jechoniah) King of Judah. |
| 597 | Jehoiachin (after three months) deposed—Zedekiah, King of Judah—Ezekiel led captive—The Great Captivity. |
| 586 | Nebuchadnezzar takes Jerusalem the third time—The City and the Temple are destroyed. |
| 561 | Evil-merodach, King of Babylon. |
| 559 | Neriglissar, King of Babylon, |
| 556 | Laborosoarchod, King of Babylon. |
| 555 | Nabonidus, King of Babylon. Belshazzar associated with Nabonidus. |
| 539 | Cyrus defeats Nabonidus. |
| 538 | Cyrus takes Babylon, and appoints "Darius the Median" (Daniel v. 31) Regent of Babylon. |
| 536 | Cyrus reigns at Babylon—Decree of Cyrus. |
| 535 | End of the Seventy Years. Subsequent rebellions of Babylon. |

---

| NEW DATE. | EVENTS, ACCORDING TO THE NEW ARRANGEMENT. |
|---|---|
| 586 | Jehoiakim, King of Judah. |
| 583 | Nineveh destroyed by the Babylonians and Medes. |
| 581 | Nebuchadnezzar, King of Babylon. |
| 575 | Jehoiachin (or Jeconiah), King of Judah. |
| 574 | Zedekiah, King of Judah. |
| 563 | Destruction of Jerusalem. |

| NEW DATE. | EVENTS, ACCORDING TO THE NEW ARRANGEMENT. |
|---|---|
| 563 .. | Commencement of the Seventy Years. |
| 538 .. | Evil-merodach, King of Babylon. |
| 535 .. | Neriglissar, King of Babylon. |
| 531 .. | Laborosoarchod, King of Babylon. |
| 530 .. | Cambyses, King of Babylon—Nabonidus appointed Viceroy. |
| 523 .. | Nabonidus revolted from Cambyses. |
| 521 .. | Darius laid claim to the throne of Babylon. |
| 513 .. | Cyrus the Second, King of Babylon—Decree of Cyrus. |
| 510 .. | Return of the first caravan of Jews. |
| 506 .. | Darius succeeded Cyrus the Second. |
| 493 .. | Darius suppressed the revolt of Belshazzar, and "took the kingdom" (Daniel v. 31). |
| 493 .. | End of the Seventy Years. |
| 486 .. | Dedication of the Temple. |
| 486 .. | Xerxes, King of Persia. |
| 484 . | Death of Darius. |

## The History of Babylon and the Jews.

### (according to the new arrangement.)

In the year 583, when *Nabopalassar* was king of Babylon and *Cyaxares I.* was king of Media, the Babylonians and Medes drove the Scythians from Asia and destroyed the city of Nineveh. From this time the *Babylonian or Chaldæan Empire* commenced its career. Although the supremacy of Asia passed away from Assyria, and was transferred first to Babylon, and afterwards to the "great kings" of the Medes and Persians : yet so great had been the glory of the "kings of Assyria," that the kings of Babylon are repeatedly called by that name, and the kings of Persia were sometimes also known by the same ancient title (Ezra vi. 22).

Soon after the destruction of Nineveh, *Nebuchadnezzar*, son of Nabopalassar defeated the invasion of

Pharaoh-Necho, king of Egypt, at Carchemish on the Euphrates. Then he conquered Syria, reduced Jehoiakim, king of Judah, to the position of a vassal of Babylon (2 Kings xxiv. 1 ; Jeremiah xlvi. 2), and marched onwards towards Egypt. Nebuchadnezzar was the commander of the Babylonian army in this campaign ; and as he is called "king" of Babylon, he is supposed to have been associated in the kingdom with his father. Nabopalassar was probably of great age, having reigned, first at Nineveh and afterwards at Babylon, for forty-five years at the time of his death.

In the year 581 Nabopalassar died, and *Nebuchadnezzar* was recalled from the Egyptian frontier to succeed his father on the throne of Babylon.

In the year 586 *Pharaoh-Necho* (Necho II), king of Egypt, had invaded the dominions of Nabopalassar, king of Babylon. *Josiah*, king of Judah, marched against the king of Egypt, but was defeated and slain at Megiddo. His successor *Jehoahaz* reigned but three months, when he was deposed by Necho, who placed *Jehoiakim* upon the throne, at the same time reducing the kingdom of Judah to the position of a tributary of Egypt. Jehoiakim reigned eleven years, until the year 575 (2 Kings xxiii. 29—36 ; 2 Chron. xxxv. 20—27 and xxxvi. 1—5). In the year 582, after the overthrow of the Scythians and the destruction of Nineveh, *Nebuchadnezzar* son of Nabopalassar turned his victorious arms against the king of Egypt who had conquered all Syria as far as the Euphrates, and defeated him at Carchemish. The Egyptians were driven out of Syria, and the whole country together with the kingdom of Judah became tributary to the Babylonian Empire (2 Kings xxiv. 1 ; Jeremiah xlvi. 2). In the space of three years, however, about the year 578 (2 Kings xxiv. 1), Jehoiakim rebelled against

Nebuchadnezzar his suzerain, and set himself up as
an independent monarch, while the Phœnicians at
the same time threw off the Babylonian yoke.
Three years passed away before Nebuchadnezzar was
prepared to reduce his rebellious subjects, until at
length in the year 575, in the third year of the reign
of Jehoiakim, counting from his reign as an independent monarch, and in the eleventh year counting from his accession to the throne, the king of
Babylon marched against him (Daniel i. 1 ; 2 Chron.
xxxvi. 5). Jerusalem was besieged and taken.
Part of the vessels of the Temple were carried to
Babylon ; and the first band of captive Jews,
amongst whom was Daniel, were led across the
Syrian desert to the banks of the Euphrates (2
Chron. xxxvi. 6—7 ; Daniel i. 2—6 ; Jeremiah lii.
28). Jehoiakim was put to death, and his son
*Jehoiachin*, or *Jeconiah*, was set upon the throne as
the vassal of Nebuchadnezzar. He almost immediately rebelled, when Nebuchadnezzar marched
again against Jerusalem. Jehoiachin gave himself
up after reigning only three months, and was carried
captive to Babylon together with all the treasures of
the Temple, in the year 574, in the eighth year of
the reign of Nebuchadnezzar. Then occurred the
Great Captivity of Judah : all the chief men were
carried away, and " none remained save the poorest
sort of the people of the land." (2 Kings xxiv. 8—
16). Over these *Zedekiah* was appointed king as
the vassal of Babylon, and he reigned for eleven
years, until the destruction of Jerusalem in 563.
The Phœnician rebellion was not so easily quelled,
for the city of Tyre did not fall till after a siege of
thirteen years. In 565, Zedekiah, forming an
alliance with Pharaoh-Hophra (or Apries), king of
Egypt, rebelled against his suzerain. The king of
Babylon marched against his unruly province. After

a long siege *Jerusalem was taken and destroyed,* in the year 563, and then commenced the *seventy years of indignation against Jerusalem.* (2 Chronicles xxxvi. 19—21 ; Zechariah i. 12). Zedekiah was punished by having his eyes put out, and by being sent to share the fate of Jehoiachin. A governor was set over the conquered province, and four years later (Jeremiah lii. 30) the last caravan of Jews was led across the Syrian desert and made to live in the populous valley of the Euphrates. After the conquest of Judæa and Phœnicia, Nebuchadnezzar turned his victorious arms against Pharaoh-Hophra, king of Egypt, whom he put to death, setting up Amasis on the throne as the vassal of Babylon.

The Prophet *Daniel* was carried captive to Babylon, as has been already mentioned, in the year 575, in the third year of the reign of Jehoiakim, counting from his revolt against Babylon and his reign as an independent monarch (Daniel i. 1). This is the explanation put upon the Book of Daniel by the "Seder Olam Rabba," one of the oldest Hebrew commentaries. From the time of his being led away in his youth until his death not earlier than 492, Daniel lived in or near the city of Babylon. The interpretation of the dream of Nebuchadnezzar took place, according to the same commentary, two years after the destruction of Jerusalem, and in the second year of the reign of Nebuchadnezzar as king over the captive Jews (Daniel ii. 1) ; and it may here be mentioned, as will be afterwards shown, that the Book of Daniel usually reckons the years of the rulers of those days from the time when they took the government over the Jewish people.* When

---

* It is probable also that in this sense the year in which Nebuchadnezzar made Jehoiakim his tributary is called by Jeremiah (xxv. 1) the first year of his reign.

Daniel had been raised to honour at Babylon, he
" continued " there during the long reign of Nebuchadnezzar and the reigns of his successors, "unto
the first year of king Cyrus." Moreover, Nebuchadnezzar made him " ruler over the whole province of
Babylon, and chief of the governors over all the
wise men of Babylon." Afterwards, during the short
reign of Belshazzar, the prophet's wonderful powers
seem to have been forgotten, until the queen-mother
reminded her son of the honours paid to Daniel by
his ancestor Nebuchadnezzar, and the prophet was
sent for to interpret the writing on the wall. Then
when Darius became king of Babylon, Daniel was
again raised to power. He "stood to confirm and
to strengthen " the new king ; and was made first of
the three presidents, who were put over the 120
prefects of the empire. For eighty-three years he
lived in the very centre of the great changes which
occurred in the East, and although quite a youth at
the time when he was taken to Babylon, he must
have been more than ninety years old at the time of
his last elevation to honour.

At Babylon, Nebuchadnezzar spared no pains to
complete the vast works in and around the huge
city ; and the mass of the captive Jews, living in
villages around, are supposed to have been employed
in these great undertakings. There happened like-
wise the wonderful events written in the Book of
Daniel, with the illness of the king, and the conse-
quent regency, and, lastly, Nebuchadnezzar's recovery.

Nebuchadnezzar is the king who is also known by
the name of Labynetus II., being the son of Labynetus I. (or Nabopalassar) and the powerful queen
Nitocris (Herodotus i, 188). Towards the end of
his reign an alliance was formed between him and
Crœsus, king of Lydia, for the purpose of resisting
the growing power of the Medes and Persians. This

great alliance against the Aryan nations is distinctly mentioned by both Herodotus and Xenophon (Herodotus i. 77 and 188 ; Xen. Cyrop. i. 5, 2—3), although both historians write very confusedly respecting the kings of Babylon, and Herodotus has not distinguished between the king who commenced the war in alliance with Crœsus and the king who was reigning at the time of the siege of Babylon. Crœsus about this time sent to consult the oracle of Delphi, and was warned that a Mule would come to make war against him (Herodotus i. 55 and 91). Nebuchadnezzar also, according to Megasthenes, when dying foretold to the Babylonians that a Persian Mule would come to put a yoke upon their necks.

In 538, *Evil-merodach* succeeded his father Nebuchadnezzar. He released the captive king Jehoiachin from his confinement, allowing him to live at the court with the honour and state of a king. Evil-merodach, continuing the alliance which had been formed by his father, joined the king of Lydia in the war against the Medes and Persians, and he is probably that "king of Assyria" who, according to Xenophon, was the ally of Crœsus king of Lydia, and who perished at the battle of Pteria in 535, when Cyrus the Second defeated Crœsus (Xen. Cyrop. iv. 1, 8).

He was succeeded by *Neriglissar* or *Nergal-share-zar*, the son-in-law of Nebuchadnezzar, and son of the regent during Nebuchadnezzar's illness. It was probably in the reign of this king that *Cyrus the Second*—at the head of the united armies of Persia and Media, and acting as the lieutenant of Cambyses, king of Persia, and Cyaxares II., king of Media—marched against Babylon for the first time. Neri-glissar, it is supposed, took the field against Cyrus, and reigned until the year 531. We are told by

Berosus that the youthful king *Laborosoarchod* succeeded Neriglissar and reigned for nine months.
He is probably the king who is related by Xenophon
to have been slain by conspirators within the city.
This conspiracy was in league with the besieging
army, and the city was taken (Xen. Cyrop. vii.
5, 30). Herodotus and Xenophon mention one long
siege of Babylon by Cyrus, when his soldiers at last
entered by marching up the bed of the Euphrates,
whose waters had been drawn off by means of canals
made above the city. But with the scanty information which we possess it is impossible to know
whether this occurred during the first capture, or
during the second fall of the city, nearly twenty
years later.

When Babylon thus fell, in 530, it came under
the dominion of *Cambyses*, king of Persia, the father
of Cyrus the Second; and *Nabonidus* (or Nabona-
dius), one of the chief conspirators, was appointed
viceroy or vassal-king.

From this time (529) dates the first year of the
reign of Cambyses as king of Babylon, and also the
first year of Nabonidus as king (or rather vassal-
king) of Babylon. Cambyses was the first of the
Persian or Achæmenian kings of Babylon; and
on the Babylonian tablets the three Achæmenian
kings—Cambyses, Cyrus, and Darius—have the
double title of "King of Babylon" and also "King
of Nations," or more correctly, "King of the Two
Nations," meaning "one of the kings of the two
confederate nations of the Persians and Medes."
This dual sovereignty of Cambyses and Nabonidus,
the one as king by right of supremacy, and the other
as his vassal reigning on the spot, may be inferred
from the tablets until 523, when Nabonidus revolted
and established his independence, while Cambyses,
being absent in Egypt from 525, was unable to

enforce the supremacy of Persia. Thus Babylon became again independent under king Nabonidus, who now assumed also the name of *Nabonidochus.* Meanwhile, as has been already mentioned, *Darius,* the son of Hystaspes, revolted from the king of Persia during his absence in Egypt, and seized the sovereignty of Persia, at the same time aiming at the possession of Babylon along with the other provinces of Cambyses. From 521 the two kings Darius and Nabonidus appear on the tablets, each claiming the title, and each in turn possessing the city until the year 517, when *Nabonidus,* having succeeded in expelling Darius, again held the undisputed severeignty. This short possession of the throne of Babylon by Darius explains also what is told us by Josephus (Antiquities x. 11, 2), that both Cyrus and Darius made war against Nabonidus.

In the year 513, in the seventeenth year of the reign of Nabonidus (as Berosus tells us), counting from 530, when Cambyses appointed him viceroy, *Cyrus the Second* made war against him. Cyrus the Second—having himself conquered Crœsus, king of Lydia, and the whole of Asia Minor, and having received the inheritance of the kingdom of Media as the dowry of his wife, the daughter of Cyaxares, as has been already told—had succeeded to the sole sovereignty of this immense dominion in the year 525 upon the death of his father-in-law, Cyaxares II. In the year 513, in the twenty-second year of his reign, counting from his conquest of Asia Minor, he undertook the conquest of Babylon for the second time, but this time he made the conquest on his own account. Nabonidus was overcome in battle, and took refuge in the fortress of Borsippa, where he surrendered. Then Cyrus commenced the long siege of Babylon. This is, perhaps, the great siege mentioned by Herodotus, who is silent about the previous conquest of the city, while Xenophon, in his account, seems to have confounded the two. The commonly-received account has been that Nabonidus, having taken refuge in Borsippa, left his son, Belshazzar, in Babylon with the queen (or queen-mother) mentioned in the Book of Daniel ; but whether this were so or not, we may consider it as certain that this was not the capture of Babylon referred to by Daniel.

The record of the conquest of Babylon by Cyrus has been preserved by tradition amongst the stories of Eastern romance.  Cyrus the First is recognised in these stories under the name of *Kai-Khosru:* while Cyrus the Second bears the name of *Coresh,* and of him it is related that he conquered Babylon and released the Jews in the days of *Gushtasp,* who was Darius, son of Hystaspes.  Thus the authority of tradition corroborates that of the Jewish historians Demetrius and Josephus, as well as of the prophet Daniel and of Megasthenes, who all lead us to suppose that Darius reigned contemporaneously with Cyrus.  Now this year, 513, is the ninth year of Darius as king of Persia, counting from his successful revolt, and the fifth year counting from the death of Pseudo-Smerdis.

And now was issued the famous *Proclamation or Decree of Cyrus* to the Jews, in the year 513, exactly fifty years after the destruction of the city of Jerusalem and the Temple of Solomon, according to the account of Josephus (against Apion i. 21), who says that the Temple of Jerusalem was desolate for fifty years.  Around the vast city Cyrus found the Jews, most of them living in villages by themselves.  The Jews, doubtless, from their never-ceasing expectation and longing to return to the land of their fathers, were looked upon by Cyrus as his natural allies against the Babylonians.  In addition to this, their superior enlightenment, and their pure, monotheistical faith, formed a great attraction to a man of such intellectual and moral capacity as Cyrus is described to have been by his biographer, Xenophon ; who, moreover, as the grandson of Cyrus the First, of the royal family of Achæmenes, belonged to the race of Persian monotheists, the servants of the Supreme Being, "Ormazd ; " and who, as the son-in-law and adopted son and successor of Ahasuerus (or Cyaxares II.), had doubtless learnt from the young queen, Esther, the Jewess, to look upon her race with favour, and had resolved to grant them the one undying longing of their hearts. This decree of Cyrus, giving orders for the rebuilding of the Temple was, however, not yet fully carried out. When Cyrus had taken possession of Babylon, he restored to the Jews the vessels of the House of God which Nebuchadnezzar had stored up in the Temple of Babylon (Ezra v. 14) ; and a large caravan of about 50,000 Jews left the land of their captivity and returned to Judæa under the leadership of Zerubbabel and Jeshua, about the year 510. But delays and difficulties prevented the complete fulfilment and realization of the wishes of Cyrus, and twenty years from the time of the decree were yet to run before the "seventy years of indignation against Jerusalem " (Zechariah i. 12) were ended. The Jews still, however, remembered the Decree of Cyrus, and twenty years later, they obtained from king Darius, as will be afterwards told, another decree in confirmation of the former.

Cyrus the Second reigned as king of Babylon (Ezra v. 13) until his death in 506. His reign counts from the year 513, when he overthrew king Nabonidus, and commenced the siege ; and thus the decree bore date the first year of Cyrus (Ezra i. 1 ; v. 13 ; vi. 3). On the Babylonian tablets he bears the

double title of "King of Babylon," and "King of the
the Two Nations." Thus, during the last seven
years of his life he was king of Babylon, and king of
Media, and of Asia-Minor, his dominions extending
from the Ægean Sea on the west to India on the
east ; while Darius, son of Hystaspes, of the younger
branch of the Persian royal family of Achæmenes, sat
upon the throne of Persia, and ruled over Syria and
Egypt. We have reason to suppose that there was
some antagonism between these two kings—the one,
the conqueror of Asia-Minor and Babylon, and the
rightful successor to the supreme rule over the
Persians and Medes ; the other claiming the supremacy by right of his successful occupation of the
imperial throne of Persia. The city of Babylon lay
on the border land between the dominions of these
two monarchs, and the tribute-tablets also allow us
to suppose that Darius claimed the title of "king of
Babylon" after this conquest. Thus probably we
may understand the account of the Mohammedan
writer, Tabari, who says that "Gouschtasp (Darius
son of Hystaspes), being displeased on hearing that
Syria and Palestine were oppressed, and Jerusalem
desolate and in ruins, sent his general Kouresh
(Cyrus) to Babylon, and ordered him to take Nabuchodonosor (Nabonidus) and send him to Balk, and at
the same time to send back the children of Israel to
Jerusalem. Kouresh (Cyrus) did as he was com-
manded, and then took the government of Babylon."
We may also suppose that Daniel refers to some
antagonism between these two kings (x. 13 and 20),
and that Daniel himself wished to return to Judæa
along with Zerubbabel (x. 1), but that he was induced
to remain in the East with Cyrus, and afterwards
with his successor, Darius (x. 13 ; xi. 1).

Cyrus the Second, as has been already mentioned,
never ruled over the imperial province of Persia, and

was by birth, marriage, adoption, and dominion, essentially a Mede; but being also the grandson of Cyrus the First, king of Persia, who had transferred the supremacy from the Medes to the Persians, and the son of Cambyses, king of Persia, who lost the supremacy during his absence in Egypt, he was the legitimate heir of the throne of his father and his grandfather, from which he was excluded by the successful usurpation of Darius. He therefore often went by the title of "king of Persia," and is so described in the Books of Daniel and Ezra. This is the reason why his name has been lost; for the historians, knowing that Cyrus, king of Persia, transferred the supremacy from the Medes to the Persians, and also knowing that the four kings of Persia—Cyrus, Cambyses, Pseudo-Smerdis, and Darius—reigned in succession, without interval, as kings of Persia, have been obliged to thrust the conquest of Babylon by Cyrus (the Second) into the reign of the first of those four kings, and have thus completely upset the sequence of events.

Here we may make mention of an inscription on a brick discovered at Warka near Babylon:—" Cyrus . . . . . . son of Cambyses the powerful . . I am he." Now this inscription speaks of Cambyses as being a powerful king; and certainly refers to Cyrus (the Second) son of that Cambyses who succeeded Cyrus the First over the confederate empire and conquered Egypt, and not to Cyrus (the First) son of a former Cambyses who is represented by Herodotus (i. 91 and 107), to have been of no great importance.

Cyrus the Second died in 506,* during one of his

---

\* Cyrus the First, being seventy years old at the time of his death (according to the Greek historian Dinon) was born in 606, and Cyrus the Second died in 506. It may be noted as strongly confirming the new chronology, that Lucian, having heard of but

occasional visits to Persia, " the seventh visit from
the acquisition of his empire," as Xenophon tells us
(Cyrop. viii. 7, 1) ; and was buried at Pasargadæ—
the old capital of the kings of Persia—where his
tomb has been indentified with the inscription, " I
am Cyrus the king, the Achæmenian." According
to the historian, Arrian, the tomb bore the words,
" I am Cyrus, the son of Cambyses, who acquired
empire for the Persians, and reigned over Asia
(the modern Asia-Minor). Grudge me not this
monument " — thus appealing to the Persians,
over whom he himself had never ruled, that they
might respect the tomb of the son of Cambyses and
the grandson of Cyrus. This interesting monument
is, doubtless, not the mausoleum of Cyrus the First,
who, according to several authorities, perished, un-
buried, far away on the field of battle, but that of
Cyrus, his grandson. Archæologists have been lately
puzzled with the Egyptian character of the sculptures
on this tomb, but this difficulty vanishes now that
we know that Cyrus the Second was the son of Cambyses, the conqueror of Egypt.

No wonder that these two great kings, one the
grandson of the other, when their deeds have been
united together as those of one prince, should have
been denominated " Cyrus the Great."

In the year 506, on the death of Cyrus the Second,
*Darius, son of Hystaspes,* of the younger branch of
the Persian royal family of Achæmenes, took possession of his dominions ; thus uniting Media, Persia,
Babylon, Egypt, Syria, and Asia-Minor, into one
great empire. From this time the name of Darius
again appears on the tablets as King of Babylon

---

one king Cyrus, says that he outlived his son Cambyses, and
lived to the age of 100 years, " as testified by the Persian and
Assyrian annals."

after an interval of twelve years (518 to 506), during which Nabonidus and Cyrus the Second had successively held the throne; and he also has the double title of "King of Babylon" and "King of the Two Nations." The years of his reign count sometimes from 521, after his successful revolt from Cambyses, and sometimes from 517, after the overthrow of Pseudo-Smerdis—a difference of four years; and on one tablet an inscription has been found of some transaction which bears a double date, both the 17th and the 13th year of Darius (the year 505).

But not even on this second accession of Darius to the throne of Babylon was he to remain in undisputed possession. The immense extent of his dominions, and the impossibility of his personal presence at more than one of his numerous capitals at the same time, made it easy for his viceroys or vassal-kings to set up an independent sovereignty. He probably attempted to rule the province as his predecessors had done by means of a tributary king, chosen from the native royal dynasty. Three times did Babylon revolt under the leadership of princes who called themselves the sons of Nabonidus. Two of these rebellions are recorded on the Behistun Rock; but that inscription appears to have been set up soon after the suppression of the second rebellion in 496, and, therefore, prior to the final fall of Babylon mentioned by Daniel. The first of these princes was *Naditabirus*, who revolted, probably, about the year 505; but, after a few years, Darius himself took Babylon and suppressed the rebellion in person. Not long afterwards, *Aracus* revolted, and Babylon was again taken. These two are amongst the nine rebellious kings who are sculptured on the Behistun Rock. After this second rebellion, *Belshazzar*, the son of Nabonidus, and probably the grandson of Nebuchadnezzar through his mother (Daniel v. 10), was appointed king, and reigned about three years. He also followed the example of his predecessors, and revolted from his suzerain ; and Darius finally took Babylon in 493, " being about threescore and two years old " (Daniel v. 31).

Herodotus mentions only one siege of Babylon by Darius, which he tells us lasted twenty months, when the Babylonians put to death nearly all the women as useless mouths, and when Darius made unsuccessful trial of the plan by which Cyrus had taken the city, at last gaining possession by means of the stratagem of Zopyrus. The history of Herodotus would lead us to suppose that this long siege occurred about the year 520, during the absence of Cambyses in Egypt, when Darius, in the course of his successful revolt, expelled Nabonidus from Babylon, and gained possession of the city for a short time. But here, again, Herodotus seems to have mixed up two or three sieges in one, for we are told by Ctesias that the taking of Babylon by means of the stratagem of Zopyrus occurred in the reign of Xerxes ; and as we know that Xerxes was associated in the kingdom with his father Darius for a considerable time— being appointed king of Egypt as early as 496—this stratagem of Zopyrus may have taken place at the time of the fall of Belshazzar.

The fall of Belshazzar is associated with the prophet Daniel, who was sent for at the instigation of the queen. Now, it has been supposed that this queen was the daughter of Nebuchadnezzar, and if so, she may have been the wife of king Neriglissar. There is evidence that Nabonidus was of the Chaldæan order, belonging to the same family to which the regent during Nebuchadnezzar's illness and king Neriglissar both belonged ; and it is not improbable that he also may have married the daughter of Nebuchadnezzar in order more firmly to secure his

throne ; in which case she may have been the mother
of Belshazzar, and considerably advanced in years at
the time of the last fall of Babylon.  The account of
the queen given by Daniel (v. 10—12), and the importance there assigned to her, allow us to suppose
that she was the daughter of the great king Nebuchadnezzar.

From this time (493) commences the third or Scrip-
tural reckoning of the years of the reign of *Darius,*
when he "was made king over the realm of the Chal-
dæans" (Daniel ix. 1), as well as of the Jews both at
Babylon and Jerusalem, and ruled over Babylon without the appointment of a native prince as viceroy.
Thus Darius united all his dominions into one great
empire, and, profiting by his own experience as well
as by that of his predecessors from the time of Nebuchadnezzar who had been troubled by so many
repeated revolts, he made some change in the ad-
ministration of the twenty great national satrapies
into which his empire had been divided, and sub-
divided it into smaller provinces ruled by the 120
"princes" mentioned by Daniel, over whom Daniel
himself was the chief "president."  We may also
suppose that Darius held Daniel in honour at the
time of some of his previous occupations of Babylon,
although we know that Darius did not always himself reside there when he came into possession of the
city.  It seems not improbable that Daniel was pro-
moted to honour by Darius when he occupied Babylon
upon the death of Cyrus the Second, in 506, and that
he also in one place calls this the first year of the
reign of Darius (Daniel xi. 1).

Now ended, in the year 493, the "*Seventy Years*"
spoken of by the Prophets.  This period of Seventy
Years has hitherto always been supposed to commence
in 605, at the time when Daniel was led to Babylon,
and to have closed in 535, the year after the Decree

of Cyrus the Great. But there is nothing in Scripture to connect the commencement of the Seventy Years with the taking of Daniel to Babylon; and there is also nothing which tells us that the Seventy Years came to an end at the time of the Decree of Cyrus. There is, however, conclusive evidence to show that this period of Seventy Years' "desolation" and "indignation" commenced with the *destruction of the City and Temple of Jerusalem* by Nebuchadnezzar (2 Chronicles xxxvi. 19-·21; Jeremiah xxv. 8—11; Daniel ix 2; Zechariah i. 12). The end of the Seventy Years we are told came to pass "in the first year of Darius," when, by his great act of humiliation and prayer, Daniel "understood by books the number of the years." So that the commencement of the Seventy Years is now thought to have occurred about the year 563, the year of the destruction of Jerusalem; and the end of the Seventy Years about the year 493, at the time of the final taking of Babylon, called by Daniel the first year and by Zechariah the second year of the reign of Darius (Daniel ix. 2; Zechariah i. 1 and 12). About this time also there went forth, as will be afterwards related, the Second Decree for the rebuilding of the Temple in confirmation of the Decree of Cyrus (Ezra vi. 6—12).

There is another consideration which may explain to us how it was that Darius was destined to carry out that great restoration of the City and Temple of Jerusalem which Cyrus had commenced. Herodotus tells us that one of the wives of Cambyses was his own sister Atossa; that afterwards Gomates the Magian (or Pseudo-Smerdis, the pretended Smerdis), who usurped the throne of Persia, obtained possession of her; and still later, when Darius overthrew Gomates, he also had Atossa as one of his wives. Herodotus, in telling his history of Atossa, calls her the daughter of

Cyrus and sister of Cambyses and Smerdis ; but she was probably the daughter-in-law of Cyrus, having been the chosen wife of his younger son Cyaxares II. (or Ahasuerus), upon whose death Cambyses probably got possession of her. She is called by the names of *Esther* the Jewess, *Hadassah* (Esther ii. 7), and *Atossa* (Herodotus). She is represented as being the mother of Xerxes the Great, as advising Darius to undertake the expedition against Greece, and as having " unbounded influence " over him (Herodotus vii. 3). The Mohammedan writer Tabari mentions a tradition that the son of Gushtasp (Darius) was born of a Jewess. Thus in the events which brought about the restoration of the Jews, we see how the prophet Daniel, during his long life, and by his talents and powers, produced an impression upon the rulers of Babylon, inclining them to regard the Jews and their religion with favour ; and now we see also how queen Esther, the wife of Ahasuerus, and afterwards of Darius, performed her part in the restoration of her countrymen, and probably influenced king Darius to issue the Second Decree confirming the First Decree of Cyrus.

Another circumstance in the reign of Darius is the final return to the predominance of Media over the sister province of Persia. The common laws of the two confederate nations are known as the " laws of the Medes and Persians," and are so mentioned in the Book of Daniel ; while at the end of the Book of Esther mention is made of the " Chronicles of the kings of Media and Persia." (Esther x. 2.) It is worthy of remark, that throughout the account of the state banquet of Ahasuerus, we find the expression " Persia and Media " three times used, and once the unusual expression, " The laws of the Persians and Medes." Now this banquet occurred about the time of the death of Cyrus the First, who

had transferred the supremacy to the Persians, and
it would seem that court etiquette had ordered that
Persia should be named before Media in order to
assert the pre-eminence which had been acquired.
Darius, however, seemed desirous of calling himself
a Mede (Daniel v. 31, xi. 1) ; and by his marriage
with the wife of Ahasuerus, king of the Medes, he
considered himself the representative of the house of
Ahasuerus, and although himself of Persian descent,
he is called " Darius, the son (or representative of
the house) of Ahasuerus, of the seed of the Medes."
(Daniel ix. 1.)   For had not the Medes been the
chief instruments in the destruction of Nineveh and
the conquest of Babylon—those two enemies by
whom the Children of Israel had been carried into
captivity ?   What greater title then could Darius
assert to the sovereignty of Babylon, than that of
being the king of Media ; and what better claim to
the friendship of the Jews than to declare himself
the successor of Ahasuerus, whose queen, Esther, had
liberated many of her kinsmen from persecution, and
whose son-in-law, Cyrus the Second, had allowed
them to return to Jerusalem ?   In addition to this,
the inscription on the Behistun Rock tells us how
Darius had to contend against rebellious princes in
Media, who asserted that they belonged to the
Median royal race of Cyaxares ; so that, in order to
strengthen his rule over the most important and
most central province of his empire, he was desirous
of representing himself as the successor of that
ancient line.   We know, too, how from this time the
Persian royal residences were abandoned, and how
the " great kings " of the Medo-Persian Empire made
Susa, Ecbatana, and sometimes Babylon, the royal
residences of the empire.   Moreover, as if still further
to show his preference for the Medes over the Persians,
Darius gave to his favourite son, the son of his

favourite wife Atossa, the name of Xerxes (in Hebrew
Ahasuerus, and in Median Cyaxares), the same name
which had been borne by the king of Media (Cyaxares I.), who, in conjunction with the king of Babylon, had overthrown the city of Nineveh--and which
had also been the name of the first husband of queen
Atossa (Cyaxares II.)*

We are told by Herodotus (i. 209) that Darius was
about twenty years old at the time of the death of
Cyrus the First (in 536), and by Daniel that he was
about sixty-two years old at the time of the final fall
of Babylon (in 493). These two statements have been
used to determine the number of years between the
two events. It has always been the custom to consider " Darius the Median" (Daniel v. 31) as the
viceroy of Cyrus the Great at Babylon, holding that
office during two years until Cyrus came to reign at
Babylon in person. If he was only a viceroy, it is
surprising that Daniel should have given us his age ;
but being the great Darius, the real founder of the
Medo-Persian Empire, and lord over the country
from the Isles of Greece to the borders of India, and
from Scythia to Æthiopia, the "great king, the
king of kings,"† from whom the coinage derived its
name, there is no wonder that the years of his life
should have been carefully recorded by both Herodotus and Daniel.

Let us now return to Judæa. The Decree of Cyrus,
giving orders for the building of the " House of the
Lord God of Israel " at Jerusalem, went forth, as has
been related, in the year 513, in the first year of the

---

* To show still further the importance which was given to this
name, we may mention that the first part of the. word Xerxes
(written on the cuneiform inscriptions " Khshayarsha ") is supposed to be perpetuated in the present title of " Shah " of Persia.

† In modern Persian the title "King of Kings" is written
" Shah-in-Shah."

reign of Cyrus the Second as "king of Babylon" (Ezra v. 13). Soon after this, probably about the year 510, the first caravan of joyful people under Zerubbabel and Jeshua returned to the land of their fathers, and in the second year of their arrival at Jerusalem the foundations of the Temple were laid. But "the people of the land weakened the hands of the people of Judah, and troubled them in building, and hired counsellors against them, to frustrate their purpose, all the days of Cyrus . . . even until the reign of Darius" (Ezra iv. 4—5).

Two kings, Ahasuerus and Artaxerxes, are mentioned in the Book of Ezra as reigning in the interval between the Decree of Cyrus and the Decree of Darius; and the commonly-accepted account of these two kings has endeavoured to identify them, in a manner which no one has ventured to consider satisfactory, with the two kings of Persia, Cambyses and Pseudo-Smerdis. There is, however, good reason for supposing that these two were either two of the sons of Darius, or else, and more probably, that they refer to one and the same son of Darius. As we have seen already, the dominions of all the ancient monarchies of the East became united under one "great king" Darius in the year 506, and again, finally, in the year 493; and being unable himself personally to inspect all the affairs of his empire, he associated his son Xerxes with himself in the government. An inscription recently discovered in Egypt leaves it pretty certain that his son Xerxes was sent to rule over Egypt as viceroy, with the title of "king," as early as the year 497—four years before the final fall of Babylon; and it is supposed that the province of Judæa, from its close proximity to Egypt, was placed under his jurisdiction.

It has been already mentioned that the names Ahasuerus and Xerxes are identical; and we have reason

to believe that Xerxes afterwards took to himself
the title of Artaxerxes, and that historians sometimes
wrote of him by this name. Thus we are told that
Ezra returned to Jerusalem in the seventh year of the
reign of Artaxerxes (Ezra vii. 8), and this was probably
the seventh year of the reign of Xerxes (the year
479), and not the seventh year of the reign of Artaxerxes Longimanus (the year 458); for Josephus tells
us (Antiquities xi. 5. 1) that Esdras (or Ezra) was
sent to Jerusalem by Xerxes, son of Darius ; and the
Septuagint translation of the Book of Daniel tells us
that " Artaxerxes of the seed of the Medes took the
kingdom, Darius being full of years and venerable
with old age," thus giving to Xerxes the name of
Artaxerxes.

We are told that the obstruction to the building
of the Temple continued "in the reign of Ahasuerus"
(Xerxes) ; and that "in the days of Artaxerxes"
(who is probably the same as Ahasuerus or Xerxes)
the enemies of the Jews wrote to "Artaxerxes, king
of Persia" (Ezra iv. 6—7). The letter to Artaxerxes
and the reply to that letter both make mention of
the "kings," and allow us to suppose that Darius had
already associated his son with himself in the empire
(Ezra iv. 13, 22). Artaxerxes, on receiving their
letter, ordered a search to be made amongst the
records of Babylon, and finding that Jerusalem had
been a most rebellious and troublesone city, he issued
an order forbidding the building. " Then ceased the
work of the house of God . . . unto the second year
of the reign of Darius," that is, until the year 491
(Ezra iv. 24). But as that time approached, Zerubbabel, the prince of the Jews, and Jeshua the high-
priest, encouraged by the words of the prophets
Haggai and Zechariah (Ezra v. 1—2), who told them
that the *Seventy Years of indignation against
Jerusalem* were now expired (Zechariah i. 12), re-

sumed the building of the Temple, and their enemies
were not able to restrain them. One last effort,
however, was made to hinder them. Now that
Babylon had fallen, and Darius "took the kingdom"
of Babylon, as well as the "kingdom" over the Jews
both at Babylon and at Jerusalem, this last appeal
against the Jews was made to him personally. In
the letter to Darius he was requested to order a
search in the "king's treasure house" at Babylon
(Ezra v. 17), in order to see if it really were true, as
the Jews constantly affirmed, that Cyrus had issued
a Decree for the building of the Temple. Then
Darius ordered a search to be made "in the house
of the rolls, where the treasures were laid up in
Babylon." The original Decree of Cyrus was not
however found in Babylon; but it was found at
Ecbatana in Media, which had been the principal
residence of Cyrus the Second (Ezra vi. 2). Then
Darius issued the *Second Decree* for the rebuilding
of the Temple (Ezra vi. 8), confirming the *First Decree*
which had been issued by Cyrus. This Second Decree
also gives us to infer that the son of Darius was associated with his father, and it seems to have borne the
joint names of *Darius and Artaxerxes* (Ezra vi. 10, 14).

Thus we see that the final fall of Babylon in the
year 493 removed all obstruction to the rebuilding of
Jerusalem, and was almost immediately followed by
the Decree of Darius. The Seventy Years of the
"desolation" of Jerusalem were now ended, and "the
reign of the kingdom of Persia" was fully established
(2 Chron. xxxvi. 20, 21). This year, 493, was exactly
*seventy weeks*, or 490 years (30 + 390 + 70), after
the dedication of the Temple of Solomon in the year
983 (1 Kings vi. 38, and xi. 42, Ezekiel iv. 1-5); and
exactly *seventy weeks* or 490 years, as Daniel also tells
us, before the Birth of Christ in B.C. 3 (Daniel ix. 24).

From this time the Jews prosecuted the work with

vigour, and about the year 486, in the sixth year of the reign of Darius, *the Second Temple* (or Temple of Zerubbabel) *was completed and solemnly dedicated* (Ezra vi. 15). In their joyful thanksgiving the Children of Israel remembered how the kings of Assyria and Babylon had led them captive over the desert of Syria into distant lands; and now they rejoiced because the Lord "had turned the heart" of the new "king of Assyria" (Ezra vi. 22), the "great king" Darius, who reigned over all the dominions of Shalmaneser, Sennacherib and Nebuchadnezzar.

From this year 486, when the Temple was completed and dedicated, the "seven weeks and threescore and two weeks"—or the 483 years—of the prophet Daniel are counted, bringing us to B.C. 3, the ordinary date of the birth of "Messiah the Prince" (Daniel ix. 25). The "seven weeks"—or 49 years—ended in the year 437, when the *Wall of Jerusalem was finished and dedicated*, and the great work of the Restoration of the Jews, which had been begun by Cyrus the Second in the year 513, received at last its complete accomplishment.

The completion of the Temple, in the year 486, was just at the close of the reign of Darius. We are told by Herodotus, Manetho, and Egyptian inscriptions, that he reigned thirty-six years; and by Ctesias (using the second reckoning of the years of his reign) that he reigned thirty-one years and died at the age of seventy-two. The years of his reign, from his successful revolt against Cambyses, count from 521, thus making his thirty-sixth year in 486; and the years of his life, reckoning him at the age of twenty on the death of Cyrus the First, in 536, make him seventy-two years old in 484.* We know also

---

* The commonly-accepted chronology of the early Persian kings, by placing the death of Cyrus the Great in the year 529, makes Darius only sixty-four when he died.

from Herodotus (vii. 1—4) that the whole care of his
vast empire was handed over before his death to his
son Xerxes, whose reign, therefore, commenced in the
year 486.

Darius was buried near Persepolis, in the here-
ditary province of Persia, the ancestral home of the
Persian royal family of Achæmenes ; and on his tomb
he is called : " Darius, the Great King, the King of
Kings ; the King of all inhabited countries ; the
King of this great earth, far and near ; the son of
Hystaspes, an Achæmenian ; a Persian, the son of a
Persian ; an Aryan, of Aryan descent."

This is not the place to discuss the intimate con-
nection between the monotheism of the Jews and
that of the Medo-Persians.  No account has come
down to us of the death of Daniel, who had been
elevated to such a pinnacle of power by the succes-
sive rulers of Babylon.  But another connecting
link between the two nations is given us in the
history of Darius written by an Arabian historian,
Abu Mohammed Mustapha.  He tells us that " after
this king had reigned thirty years (about the year
491 or 487 according to the different reckonings of
his reign) Zerdust (Zoroaster) appeared—a wise
man who was author of the books of the Magi.  At
first Gushtasp (Darius, son of Hystaspes) was dis-
inclined to the new doctrine, but at length was per-
suaded, and adopted his religion.  He was among
the disciples of Ozier (Ezra ?)."  The lapse of ages
has not swept away the religion of the followers of
Ezra, nor that of the followers of Zoroaster; although
the destruction of Jerusalem in A.D. 70, and the
overthrow of the dynasty of the Sassanidæ by the
Mohammedan conquerors of Persia, in A.D. 652, have
sent them both as exiles from their native land.

The question will now be asked :—Ought not Herodotus and Xenophon to have known better than to write with such discrepancy respecting the foundation of the Medo-Persian Empire, seeing that when dealing with Grecian history their trustworthiness is undisputed ? The answer to this is given by the historians themselves. Herodotus says : "I shall follow those Persians who do not wish to magnify the actions of Cyrus, but to relate the plain truth ; though I am aware that there are three other ways of relating Cyrus's history ;" and when relating the death of Cyrus, he says : " Of the many accounts given of the end of Cyrus this appears to me most worthy of credit." Xenophon also confesses to much difference in the authorities from which he derived his history, even in the matter of the princess whom Cyrus married. It has been shown how Cyrus the First was entirely of Persian descent, while his grandson Cyrus the Second was essentially a Mede ; and Herodotus seems to have heard most of the Persian king, while Xenophon relates chiefly the history of the Mede.

———
.

Harrison and Sons, Printers in Ordinary to Her Majesty, St. Martin's Lane.